D0436406

Over the Moon!

Adapted by Geof Smith
Based on the screenplay "Help the Cow" by Susan Kim
Illustrated by Kellee Riley

 A GOLDEN BOOK • NEW YORK

www.randomhouse.com/kids
ISBN: 978-0-375-86567-1
Printed in the United States of America
10 9 8 7 6 5 4 3

It was a quiet night in the classroom. Linny the Guinea Pig, Turtle Tuck, and Ming-Ming the Duckling were getting ready for bed. Suddenly, the phone rang.

"The phone is ringing!" cried Linny.
"There's an animal in trouble somewhere,"
said Tuck.

"Look!" said Linny. "That little cow is calling because she can't jump."

"But why would a cow want to jump?" asked Ming-Ming.

Linny thought for a moment. "She must be the cow from the nursery rhyme. You know . . ."
"'Hey diddle diddle,
The cat and the fiddle,

The cow jumped over the moon.

The little dog laughed to see such sport.

And the dish ran away with the spoon.'"

"We have to help the little cow!" declared Ming-Ming. But when the Wonder Pets started to build the Flyboat, they discovered that the flying disc was high up on a shelf and no one could reach it. Linny had an idea.

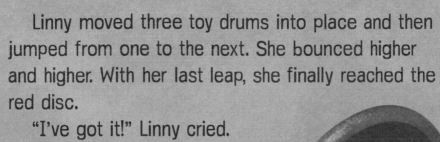

Linny moved three toy drums into place and then jumped from one to the next. She bounced higher and higher. With her last leap, she finally reached the red disc.

"I've got it!" Linny cried.

With the red disc—and teamwork—the Wonder
Pets finished building the Flyboat.

"But, Linny, where do jumping cows live?"
asked Tuck.

"In Mother Goose Land," Linny replied. "We
have to fly into this book of nursery rhymes."

The Flyboat took off, and the Wonder Pets flew into the open book.

"We're coming to save you, Little Cow!" Ming-Ming shouted.

As the Wonder Pets soared through the pages
of the book, they saw Mother Goose and Little
Miss Muffet.

At last the Wonder Pets found Little Cow. She looked very sad.

"We're here to put some pump in your jump," declared Ming-Ming.

Little Cow wasn't the only one who was sad.
Until she jumped, the dog couldn't laugh, the
dish couldn't run away with the spoon, and the
cat and the fiddle didn't know what to do!

"But cows don't have wings," said Linny.
The Wonder Pets needed another plan.

Luckily, Tuck had an idea. "Maybe the cow can bounce, like Linny did in the classroom," he said.

"The drums are back at school. But maybe Little Cow can jump on these mushrooms," Linny suggested. "They're very bouncy."

Little Cow wasn't too sure. She thought the mushrooms looked very wobbly.

"Don't worry," said Linny. "We'll jump with you. Teamwork always does the trick!"

So they all jumped and jumped and jumped.
Then—with a big, bouncy jump—the cow leaped
over the moon!

"That's one small step for nursery rhymes, but one giant leap for me," said Little Cow.

Everyone cheered! The cat played the fiddle.
The little dog laughed. And the dish ran away
with the spoon.

"Wonder Pets, we'd like to thank you," said the laughing dog. "Here's a tisket, a tasket, a yummy celery-filled basket!"

"That cow really can jump," said Linny. "It looks like our work here is done, Wonder Pets!"